Kamik
an Inuit Puppy Story

Published by Inhabit Media Inc.
www.inhabitmedia.com

Inhabit Media Inc. (Iqaluit), P.O. Box 11125, Iqaluit, Nunavut, X0A 1H0
(Toronto), 146A Orchard View Blvd., Toronto, Ontario, M4R 1C3

Design and layout copyright © 2012 Inhabit Media Inc.
Text copyright © 2012 Donald Uluadluak
Illustrations copyright © 2012 Qin Leng

Editors: Neil Christopher, Louise Flaherty, and Kelly Ward
Art Director: Danny Christopher

We acknowledge the financial support of the Government of Canada through the Department of Canadian Heritage Canada Book Fund.

We acknowledge the support of the Canada Council for the Arts for our publishing program.

Printed in Canada

Library and Archives Canada Cataloguing in Publication

Uluadluak, Donald
    Kamik : an Inuit puppy story / adapted from the memories
of Donald Uluadluak ; Illustrated by Qin Leng.

ISBN 978-1-927095-11-9

    1. Sled dogs--Juvenile fiction. I. Leng, Qin II. Title.

PS8641.L82K36 2012   jC813'.6   C2012-905723-1

Kamik
an Inuit Puppy Story

Adapted from the memories of **Donald Uluadluak**

Illustrated by **Qin Leng**

INHABIT
MEDIA

"Ataatasiaq? Are you home?" Jake called as he walked into his grandfather's kitchen. He kicked his snowy boots onto the rubber mat and left the door open for Kamik, his puppy, to come inside the house.

"Hello," Jake's grandfather called from the sitting room. "Come on in, but close the door. It's cold."

Jake turned to look for Kamik in the doorway, but all he saw of the little dog was his tail scampering back down the steps and around the side of the house.

"Kamik! Get back here!" Jake called after his dog. "He never listens to me, Ataatasiaq!"

Jake hopped down the steps in his socks and pulled Kamik from under the porch.

Back inside the house, Kamik squirmed and wiggled, trying to get out of Jake's arms.

"Stop it. Stay," Jake said, sternly. But Kamik finally freed himself and ran through the kitchen, leaving little, wet pawprints on the floor.

"Kamik. Come." Jake's commands were of no use. Kamik ran around the sitting room in circles, until he finally came to rest in a warm spot next to Jake's grandfather's feet.

"He's certainly full of energy," Jake's grandfather said with a laugh.

"He never listens, no matter how loud I yell. I called him Kamik because his fur looks like he's wearing a boot. I should have called him Bad Dog."

Jake's grandfather looked down at the restless puppy that was gently chewing on the base of his armchair.

"When I was raising dogs, we used to name our puppies after older dogs who had passed away. I named my puppies after strong dogs my grandfather used in his dog teams. Some of the names had been passed down since before I was born."

"Your grandmother was a great dog trainer, Jake. She and the other women from our camp helped raise many good dogs.

"I remember my own grandmother speaking to the puppies as she stretched their muscles, telling them to be strong, ambitious, and obedient to their masters. Dogs can understand more of what we say than you can imagine. Your grandmother loved her dogs. She raised them in a similar way to raising a child."

"In order to train a good dog, you have to build trust with the dog, living with it every day and teaching it through how you behave and how you treat it.

"I spent a lot of time with my dogs. It was more like building a good friendship than raising an animal. Eventually they start to understand you and you start to understand them."

"When you train a dog well, he can become a very reliable and dependable helper. I relied on my dogs all the time when I travelled with them out on the land."

Jake smiled at the thought of travelling by dog team across the tundra. It would be a lot faster than riding his old hand-me-down bike.

"I can't wait to take out my own dog team!" Jake exclaimed. "I'm going to outrun all my friends with my super fast dogs!"

Jake ran around the room pretending to race his qamutik across the land. Kamik barked excitedly from where he sat on the floor.

Jake's grandfather smiled.

"**When I hunted by dog team,** my dogs were my constant helpers.

"Once, I got caught in a terrible blizzard. The weather was so bad that I couldn't even see the dogs in front of the qamutik.

"But I knew that once a dog has taken a trail, he knows that trail and will never get lost, so I trusted my dogs to find their way home.

"When the dogs suddenly stopped, I ran to them to see what was the matter. They had stopped because we were home. We were right in front of our own porch!

"If I had been alone, I would never have made it home."

"Dogs can also sense dangers that people cannot see. They can warn us about thin ice and the presence of dangerous animals.

"My dogs once even saved my life by waking me when a fire broke out in my camp at night."

"Well-trained dogs can help their masters all year long.

"In the summer, my dogs would help me pull out tent poles that were stuck deep in the earth.

"Once, when I didn't have a motor for my boat, I tied my dogs to the boat with long ropes and they ran along the shore, pulling my boat through the water just as if I had a motor.

"For ten years I hunted by dog team and my dogs helped me that entire time. They found foxholes for me and could smell and hear caribou much better than any person could."

"When the hunt was over and we were on our way home—even though the dogs were tired from long days of watching for danger and pulling my sled—they always seemed happier than ever to be returning to camp.

"They pulled faster and ran harder on the way home.

"I think it was because they knew they would be returning to your grandmother and the other women who cared about them and had loved them from the time they were puppies even smaller than Kamik here."

Kamik had drifted off to sleep in a patch of sunlight at Jake's grandfather's feet. Jake looked at his big puppy paws and wondered how long it would be before he was strong enough and smart enough to be a sled dog.

"Jake?" Jake's mom called to him from the front door. "It's time to come home for supper."

Jake got up and thanked his grandfather for telling him about his dogs. He moved to the other side of the room and called for Kamik to follow him. Kamik didn't move. Jake called three more times, but Kamik stayed put.

"I don't think he wants to go!" Jake's grandfather said with a chuckle.

Jake let out an exhausted sigh and ran over to pick up Kamik and take him home.

Just before leaving the room, Jake turned to look at his grandfather.

"Ataatasiaq, what did you call your lead dog when you had a dog team?"

"Her name was Tuhaaji," Jake's grandfather replied. "She was a very smart dog."

As Jake left the room, his grandfather heard him whisper to his puppy, "Come on, Tuhaaji, you and I are going to need to spend a lot more time together from now on."

Donald Uluadluak is an elder from Arviat, Nunavut. He was born and raised on the land by his grandparents, when Inuit were nomadic and depended on game for survival. He was an elder advisor for the Nunavut Department of Education for several years. Recently he retired and began recording memories and recollections from his life to publish as books for future generations. *Kamik: An Inuit Puppy Story* is the first book to be based on these fond memories. He has a lot more to contribute that the younger generation must learn and pass on.

Qin Leng was born in Shanghai and lived in France and Montreal. She now lives and works as a designer and illustrator in Toronto. Her father, an artist himself, was a great influence on her. She grew up surrounded by paintings, and it became second nature for her to express herself through art. She graduated from The Mel Hoppenheim School of Cinema and has received many awards for her animated short films and artwork. Qin Leng always loved to illustrate the innocence of children and has developed a passion for children's books. She has published numerous picture books in Canada, the United States, and South Korea.

Iqaluit · Toronto
www.inhabitmedia.com